CLASSIC STARTS™

The Phantom of the Opera

Retold from the Gaston Leroux original by Diane Namm

Illustrated by Troy Howell

STERLING

New York / London
www.sterlingpublishing.com/kids

STERLING and the distinctive Sterling logo
are registered trademarks of Sterling Publishing Co., Inc.

Library of Congress Cataloging-in-Publication Data

Namm, Diane.
  The phantom of the opera / retold from Gaston Leroux original; abridged
by Diane Namm; illustrated by Troy Howell; afterword by Arthur Pober.
    p. cm. — (Classic starts)
  Summary: Under the Paris Opera House lives a disfigured musical genius who
uses music to win the love of a beautiful opera singer.
  ISBN-13: 978-1-4027-4580-5
  ISBN-10: 1-4027-4580-X
  [1. Horror stories.] I. Howell, Troy, ill. II. Leroux, Gaston, 1868–1927. Fantôme de
l'Opéra. English. III. Title.

PZ7.N14265Ph 2008
[Fic]—dc22

                                                        2007003946

2 4 6 8 10 9 7 5 3 1

Published by Sterling Publishing Co., Inc.
387 Park Avenue South, New York, NY 10016
Copyright © 2008 by Diane Namm
Illustrations copyright © 2008 by Troy Howell
Distributed in Canada by Sterling Publishing
^c/o Canadian Manda Group, 165 Dufferin Street,
Toronto, Ontario, Canada M6K 3H6
Distributed in the United Kingdom by GMC Distribution Services,
Castle Place, 166 High Street, Lewes, East Sussex, England BN7 1XU
Distributed in Australia by Capricorn Link (Australia) Pty. Ltd.
P.O. Box 704, Windsor, NSW 2756, Australia

Classic Starts is a trademark of Sterling Publishing Co., Inc.

Printed in China
All rights reserved

Sterling ISBN-13: 978-1-4027-4580-5
ISBN-10: 1-4027-4580-X

For information about custom editions, special sales, premium and
corporate purchases, please contact Sterling Special Sales
Department at 800-805-5489 or specialsales@sterlingpublishing.com.

CONTENTS

Pronunciation Guide 1

CHAPTER 1:

The Beginning 2

CHAPTER 2:

Is It the Ghost? 4

CHAPTER 3:

The Newest Opera Star 8

CHAPTER 4:

The Mystery Guest 15

CHAPTER 5:

Box Five 19

CHAPTER 6:

The Angel of Music 24

CHAPTER 7:

The Angel Is Revealed 29

CHAPTER 8:

The Opera Ghost's Warning 34

CHAPTER 9:

The Night of the Chandelier 39

CHAPTER 10:

Christine Disappears 44

CHAPTER 11:

At the Masked Ball 49

CHAPTER 12:

The Secret Engagement 57

CHAPTER 13:

Christine's Story 63

CHAPTER 14:

The Two Brothers Fight 70

CHAPTER 15:

Christine Disappears Again! 72

CHAPTER 16:

The Managers Behave Strangely 74

CHAPTER 17:

A Mysterious Foreign Stranger 77

CHAPTER 18:

The Police Accuse Count Philippe 80

CHAPTER 19:

Through the Looking Glass 84

CHAPTER 20:

Into the Darkness 90

CHAPTER 21:

The Room of Mirrors 97

CHAPTER 22:

Trapped! 103

CHAPTER 23:

The Intruders Are Discovered! 109

CHAPTER 24:

Room of Mirrors, Room of Illusions 113

CHAPTER 25:

Out of the Forest and Into the Desert 116

CHAPTER 26:

The Grasshopper or the Scorpion? 121

CHAPTER 27:

The Monster's Trick 126

CHAPTER 28:

The Foreign Stranger Survives 128

CHAPTER 29:

The Ghost's Love Story Ends 133

CHAPTER 30:

The Author Explains All Things 138

What Do *You* Think? 142

Afterword 145

Classic Starts Library 149

Pronunciation Guide
to the Characters

~∽~

*T*he *Phantom of the Opera* contains many French names that may be difficult to read. Here's a list that will help you learn how to pronounce them.

Christine **Daae**: Die-*ay*

Meg **Giri**: *Gee*-ree

Raoul Chagney: Rah-*ool* Shan-*yee*

Philippe Chagney: Fill-*eep* Shan-*yee*

Joseph **Buquet**: Boo-*kay*

Mr. **Poligny**: Pol-lin-*yee*

Mr. **Moncharmin**: Mon-shar-*man*

Mr. **Mifroid**: Me-*fwah*

CHAPTER 1

The Beginning

The long-ago mysteries of the great opera house in Paris have never been explained. Why did so many terrible tragedies happen there? Why did everyone flee from it in fear? Why was it left to rot, unused and empty for so many years?

I, alone, know the answer.

There is no doubt. There was a ghost in the opera house. He was real.

How do I know?

I have spoken with those who lived and

worked there long ago. I have searched the ruins of the opera house. I have found its buried secrets.

I thank all the people who have helped me on my search. Now it is time for me to tell you the truth.

CHAPTER 2

Is It the Ghost?

It was evening, and Christine Daae was singing on stage at the opera house. There was to be a party after the show for the old managers. They were tired of running the opera house. They wanted to retire. This was their last night at the opera.

The dancers were in their dressing room while Christine sang. Suddenly, the littlest one rushed in and cried, "It's the ghost! I've seen him!"

Sorelli, the oldest dancer, did not believe her. But then the rest of the dancing girls spoke.

"We have seen him, too!" they said. "We were simply too afraid to tell."

"What did he look like?" asked Sorelli.

All the dancers talked together. The ghost had appeared as a gentleman in formal clothes. He would arrive suddenly in a hallway. He seemed to come straight through the walls.

"I don't believe you!" said Sorelli.

Then the chief stagehand at the opera house stepped forward. His name was Joseph Buquet.

"I have seen him, too," Joseph said.

Everyone grew quiet.

"He is very thin. His coat hangs off his ragged frame. His eyes are like two black holes in his skull. His skin is a nasty yellow color. It is tightly stretched across his face. The worst thing of all—there is a space where his nose should be."

"Joseph! My mother says you should not talk of such things!" said little Meg Giry. Meg was the young daughter of Mrs. Giry, who was in charge of the private boxes. "It will bring you bad luck!"

Joseph lowered his head and left the room.

"Well, a fire inspector told me that he saw the ghost, too," whispered another dancer. "It had no body at all. Just a head of fire!"

"Gabriel, the choirmaster, saw the head of fire, too!" said one of the others. "It was right behind the Foreign Stranger!"

The old managers always turned to the Foreign Stranger when odd things happened at the opera house. No one knew exactly what his connection was to the ghost, but since he kept mainly to himself, they called him the Foreign Stranger.

"You know nothing about the ghost!" said little Meg Giry.

The other dancers turned to her at once.

"Tell us what *you* know," Sorelli demanded.

"Only if you can keep a secret," Meg replied.

The dancers agreed.

"My mother is in charge of the ghost's private box in the opera," Meg told them. "The ghost is never seen. He does not have a coat or a head of fire. Mother never sees him, but she hears him."

Just then they heard a noise in the hall. Sorelli crept slowly toward the door, opened it, and saw—nothing!

Then they all heard a man scream.

CHAPTER 3

The Newest Opera Star

The audience at the opera house was clapping loudly for Christine Daae. She was new at the opera and was filling in for La Carlotta, the star singer who was sick.

Where have the managers been keeping this girl? the audience wondered. *Why have we never heard her beautiful voice before?*

"She sings like an angel," Count Philippe Chagny said to his younger brother Raoul.

Raoul's strong, handsome face was quite pale.

"It can't be! It's Christine, the little girl I once knew at the shore!" Raoul said.

Then without warning, Christine fainted. The singers carried her offstage to her dressing room, as the audience left.

Raoul was very upset.

"Brother, what is it?" asked Count Philippe. "You look like you've seen a ghost!"

"I've seen a ghost from the past. Don't you remember her, brother? I must speak with her," Raoul said.

"Who?" asked Count Philippe.

"Please, brother. We must go backstage. I must see Christine—at once!" Raoul said.

Count Philippe led the way backstage. Raoul hurried behind him. On their way, they passed Sorelli and the other dancers, in a hurry to get to the opera house party in the grand lobby.

Raoul heard one of them say something

about a terrible accident. Afraid for Christine, Raoul rushed past his brother. He went straight to Christine's dressing room.

There Raoul found Christine. Her dressing room was richly decorated. It had heavy velvet drapes, a plush sofa, and several gas-light lamps. A tall, dark mirror hung on the wall. Christine lay on the sofa amid a pile of pillows. A doctor was by her side.

"Christine!" Raoul called to her.

Christine turned at the sound of her name. Her skin was as smooth as a doll's. Her hair was a mass of thick, dark curls spread out against the pillows. Her eyes looked like deep black pools. Christine stared at Raoul's worried face.

"Sir, who are you?" Christine asked in a weak whisper.

Raoul knelt beside her. He took her small, soft hand in his.

"I am the little boy who went into the sea to rescue you. Don't you remember?" Raoul asked. "Please let me speak with you privately," he added.

Christine's face went very white, as if she too had seen a ghost.

"I do not remember, you, sir. I'm sorry. I am feeling much better now. Please leave me alone," she said with a wave of her hand.

Raoul turned red with shame. He and the doctor left the room. Christine closed the door behind them.

Slowly, Raoul started down the hall. Then he stopped and looked back. He would not leave until he had spoken with Christine again.

Raoul returned to her dressing room door. He was just about to knock when he heard voices from inside.

"Christine, I am your Angel of Music. You must love only me!" Raoul heard a ghostly voice say.

"I *sing* only for you," Christine said sadly. "Isn't that enough?"

Her voice trembled with tears.

"You gave me a wonderful gift tonight, my dear. You sang beautifully," the voice said.

Raoul heard nothing more.

Several minutes later, Christine came out of her dressing room. She was wrapped in furs, and her face was hidden by a lace veil. Christine ran out of the opera house. She did not even see Raoul on the other side of her doorway.

Raoul waited. No one else came out of the dressing room. Raoul wanted to see who had claimed Christine's love. He opened the door and went into the dressing room.

Raoul was in complete darkness.

"Is someone there?" Raoul called out. His voice shook. "Why are you hiding?" he asked.

All was dark and silent.

"You are a coward!" Raoul said.

Raoul lit a lamp. There was no one there!

Am I going mad? Raoul wondered. *Was it a ghost's voice I heard?*

Raoul walked through the opera house confused. Then he heard a noise. He followed the noise to the backstage exit. There was a crowd at the door. Raoul saw an ambulance stretcher with someone on it.

"What has happened? Who is that?" he asked someone in the crowd.

"It is Joseph Buquet, the chief stagehand," someone said. "He has had a terrible accident."

"Will he be all right?" Raoul asked.

"Never again," someone else answered.

Raoul took off his hat and let the ambulance stretcher pass.

CHAPTER 4

The Mystery Guest

∽

The party for the managers in the grand lobby of the opera house was the best anyone could remember. In the middle of the noisy celebration, the littlest dancer pointed into the crowd.

"The opera ghost! The opera ghost!" she cried out.

Everybody laughed. No one believed in something they could not see.

At the retirement dinner for the new managers later that evening, there was a lot of talk and laughter. The old managers were happy to be done with the theater. They were glad to leave behind the opera ghost and his many demands.

The new managers thought the stories about a ghost were funny. They didn't believe the old managers at all.

Just then, Mr. Poligny, one of the old managers, pointed to a guest at the end of the table.

"Look!" he cried.

There sat the ghost, as natural as could be. He didn't eat or drink. He looked dark and gloomy, with deep, hollow eyes. His nose, if you could call it that, was almost invisible. Those who dared to look at him turned away after one glance.

"Gentlemen! Let the terrible tragedy of Joseph Buquet be a warning to you," the ghost said to the new managers.

Then, the opera ghost was gone!

"What does the man mean?" asked the tiny

Mr. Moncharmin, one of the new opera house managers.

"That was no man," said Mr. Poligny.

He presented a notebook to the new managers.

"What is this?" asked the tall Mr. Richard. He was the other new manager.

"The ghost's demands," said Mr. Poligny.

Mr. Moncharmin opened the notebook. On the page was red, messy writing.

Mr. Richard read the note aloud.

These are my demands:

1. By the middle of each month, you must pay me twenty thousand francs. Do not be late!

2. For every performance, you must leave Box Five empty. Only I, the opera ghost, may sit there.

After a moment, Mr. Moncharmin and Mr. Richard began to laugh. Others joined in.

"Thank you, Gentlemen. That was a very good joke," said Mr. Moncharmin.

"It is no joke," said Mr. Poligny. "If you do not do as the ghost wishes, disaster will follow."

"Well, we are not afraid of this opera ghost. We will not pay any ghost or man twenty thousand francs a month," said Mr. Moncharmin.

"And we will sell the seats in Box Five!" Mr. Richard declared.

CHAPTER 5

Box Five

୧

The new managers of the opera house, Mr. Moncharmin and Mr. Richard, were true to their word. Night after night, every seat was sold, including the seats in Box Five.

The opera house was making lots of money. La Carlotta, the star singer, was very popular with the public. Everyone wanted to hear her sing. There had been no disasters. Mr. Moncharmin and Mr. Richard were thrilled.

The new managers forgot all about the opera ghost and his demands, until Mr. Moncharmin found an envelope on his desk one morning. He recognized the red ink and the handwriting. He showed it to Mr. Richard.

"Perhaps the old managers have sent it as a joke," Mr. Richard said.

Mr. Moncharmin quickly opened the letter.

Dear Managers,

I know you are very busy men. It is not for me to tell you how to run your business. But you must know that La Carlotta sings like a toad.

I suggest that Christine Daae perform in place of La Carlotta. Remember her success when La Carlotta was sick?

I remind you that Box Five is mine. I was very upset to find others in it. If you wish to live in peace, do not take away my private box again.

Your humble servant,

The Opera Ghost

Mr. Moncharmin wrote an angry note to Mr. Poligny, the old manager.

If you wish to have free seats at the opera house tonight, you simply have to ask. Box Five is yours. You do not have to send a letter or pretend to be a ghost.

Mr. Poligny sent back a note of his own.

I wrote no such letter. I do not wish to attend the opera, not tonight or any night! I remind you that Box Five belongs to the Opera Ghost.

Mr. Moncharmin crumpled this note and threw it away.

That evening the seats in Box Five were sold. La Carlotta performed her usual starring role. Christine sang only a very small part and was hardly on stage at all. Everyone agreed, however, that Christine was a much greater success than La Carlotta.

Only one thing upset the performance. The patrons in Box Five would not be quiet. They yelled. They argued. They claimed that an invisible voice told them the box was taken. Of course, no one was there. They demanded their money back and would not leave without it.

After the show, Mr. Moncharmin stormed into his office. He sent for Mrs. Giry, the manager of the private boxes.

Mrs. Giry hurried in. She wore a faded shawl, worn shoes, an old silk dress, and a hat with three wilted feathers.

"How could this problem in Box Five happen?" Mr. Moncharmin demanded. "It is your job to look after the people who sit in the boxes!"

"It was the opera ghost," Mrs. Giry told him. "Those people were in his private box."

Mr. Moncharmin banged his fist on his desk.

"Who is this opera ghost?" he snarled. "Have you ever seen him?"

"I have not seen him, Sir, but I have heard him. He usually comes in the middle of the first act. He gives three little taps on the door. He has a low voice, soft and kind. Sometimes he asks for a footstool.

"At the end of every show, he leaves me two francs, sometimes more, on the little shelf in the box. One night, when I returned his opera glasses, he left me a box of candy," Mrs. Giry told him.

Mr. Moncharmin struck the desk again with his fist.

"We will look into the matter of Box Five for ourselves," he said. "As for you, Mrs. Giry, you are fired!"

CHAPTER 6

The Angel of Music

֍

After that night, despite her great success, Christine would not perform. She seemed afraid. She went nowhere. She saw no one. It was as if she were taking orders from someone. But who?

Raoul Chagny wrote her many notes. Again and again he asked Christine to meet him. He received no reply. Raoul was afraid he would never see Christine again. At last, however, she sent him a note.

Sir,

I remember the little boy who went into the sea to rescue me. I remember how we played together all that summer. I remember, too, that your much older brother, Philippe, did not want us to be friends. You are a Count, and I am just a poor musician's daughter.

Do you remember my father? Tomorrow is the anniversary of his death. I am going today to our little town by the sea to honor him. Do you remember meeting him? My father lies near the place where as children we kissed good-bye for the last time before Philippe took you away.

There was nothing more to the note.

Raoul raced to the train station. He jumped on the train going to Christine's seaside town just as the train was leaving.

He thought about Christine's father. What a

sweet and funny man he had been. Raoul remembered that Christine had loved her father very much. Christine's mother had passed on when Christine was just six years old.

After her mother's death, Christine's father became ill. He was not able to care for Christine on his own.

The great Valerius family from Paris admired Mr. Daae's musical talent. They agreed to care for him and to adopt Christine so they could all be together.

When he was feeling well, Christine's father spent hours playing his violin and teaching Christine to sing.

One day, however, he became very ill.

Professor and Mrs. Valerius brought Christine and her sick father to a little town by the sea. The doctors had told them that fresh air and salt water would cure Mr. Daae.

Raoul and his family were on summer vacation

there as well. While collecting shells along the shore, Raoul heard Christine sing for the very first time. He could not tear himself away from the little girl with the pure, sweet voice.

After Christine's lesson, he saw her run into the water and tumble under a wave. Mr. Daae was too weak to save her, so Raoul dove in and pulled her out.

For the rest of that summer, Christine and Raoul played together every day. Mr. Daae gave Raoul violin lessons. Afterward, Mr. Daae would tell them both wonderful stories. Christine's favorite story was about a musical angel, whose beautiful song was heard only by a lucky few.

"You will hear him one day, my child," Christine's father told her. "When I am gone, I will send him to you."

Christine's father had now been gone for several years. Christine had been living with Mrs. Valerius, who was now very old and alone.

When Raoul remembered these happy times, he could not understand what had happened at the opera. Why had Christine pretended not to know him? They had loved each other as children. Raoul loved her now. He wanted Christine to love him again.

While he was thinking about all this, the train reached Christine's town and came to a stop. Raoul leaped off. He had to find Christine and tell her what was in his heart.

CHAPTER 7

The Angel Is Revealed

❦

In the sitting room of a small inn, Raoul found Christine.

"Ah," Christine said without surprise. "The angel said you would come."

"Angel?" Raoul asked. "Did this angel also tell you that I love you, Christine? I have loved you since we were children. Now that I have found you again, I want us to marry!"

Christine blushed. Then she laughed at him.

Raoul's feelings were hurt. He was angry.

"Why do you act this way?" Raoul asked.

He did not wait for Christine to answer.

"It is because of someone else, isn't it? Someone who was in your dressing room the night I came to you," Raoul said.

Christine grew still and very pale. Dark rings formed around her eyes.

"You heard someone in my dressing room?" Christine whispered.

"I heard every word," Raoul told her.

Christine gasped.

"I thought I was the only one who could hear the voice," she said.

Two tears rolled down her cheeks.

"What is it?" Raoul asked. "What is wrong?"

Christine leaned forward.

"I will tell you a secret," she said. "The Angel of Music that my father used to tell us about has visited me. It was his heavenly voice that you heard in my dressing room."

Raoul searched Christine's face. She really

believed what she was saying. Raoul could not help himself.

"I think your 'angel' is a demon," Raoul said. "I love you, Christine, I want to marry you, please listen to me."

Christine looked past Raoul and turned pale.

"Leave me at once!" she cried, and ran up the stairs of the inn.

Christine locked herself in her room. She would not see Raoul.

Raoul would not leave without speaking with Christine once more. He decided to wait until she came out.

A little before midnight, when everyone was fast asleep, Christine slipped out of the inn. Raoul saw her white form in the moonlight. He followed her to the churchyard where her father rested in peace.

Christine seemed not to notice him. She seemed to be in a trance.

At the stroke of midnight, Raoul heard a voice singing. It was a song that Mr. Daae used to play on his violin. The voice was far sweeter, richer, and more perfect than any that Raoul had heard before. Yet, he saw no one but Christine.

When the singing stopped, Christine returned to the inn, as if in a daze.

Raoul waited to see if the singer would appear. Soon Raoul saw a shadow glide along a wall. He was sure it was the demon from the opera house. It must have followed her from Paris. It was following her still. Raoul would not allow it to harm Christine. He ran up and took hold of its cloak.

The moonlight revealed the shadow's head. The last thing Raoul remembered seeing was a snarling face and a pair of scorching eyes.

The innkeeper found Raoul the next morning. He lay half-frozen upon the inn's steps.

CHAPTER 8

The Opera Ghost's Warning

When the opera house was empty, Mr. Moncharmin and Mr. Richard searched Box Five from top to bottom, looking to see if they could find any trace of the ghost. In the gloomy half-light, they crawled upon the carpet. They poked under every red velvet cover. They sat in every seat. They peeked behind every curtain.

For a moment, they thought they saw a shape in the box.

Mr. Moncharmin and Mr. Richard stood still

and stared. In the next moment, the figure had disappeared.

"Did you see what I saw?" Mr. Moncharmin asked.

"I saw a head resting on the ledge of the box," said Mr. Richard.

"I saw the shape of an old woman," said Mr. Moncharmin.

"That settles it! Neither of us saw the same thing. There is no ghost at all!" Mr. Richard declared.

"We should sit in Box Five ourselves this very night," Mr. Moncharmin announced.

The two new managers agreed. They returned to their office. There they found another red-lettered envelope.

"This joke must end!" Mr. Richard declared. Angrily, he opened the letter and read it aloud.

My Dear Managers:

So it is to be war between us?

If you still care for peace, here are my four conditions:

1. Give me back Box Five from this day forward.

2. Christine Daae will perform tonight. La Carlotta will be ill.

3. Take back the loyal and good servant Mrs. Giry.

4. Give your letter accepting my demands to Mrs. Giry. She will deliver it to me.

Do not refuse me. Take my advice and be warned in time.

The Opera Ghost

Just then, Mr. Mercier, the assistant manager entered the office.

"A white horse from the opera stable has been stolen!" Mr. Mercier announced.

"Who is the thief?" Mr. Moncharmin asked the assistant manager.

"The opera ghost!" answered Mr. Mercier.

At that moment, Mrs. Giry rushed in.

"Do you have a letter for the opera ghost, Sir? He sent me a note tonight to tell me to collect it and bring it to him," Mrs. Giry said.

Mr. Richard's face turned bright red.

"I am sick of this opera ghost!" shouted Mr. Richard.

Mr. Richard twirled about. Before Mrs. Giry knew what was happening, Mr. Richard pushed her right out the door. She landed on her black silk skirt.

Mrs. Giry stormed off down the hall. She was so angry that the wilted feathers in her hat stood straight on end.

At the same time, La Carlotta received a red-lettered note at her home.

If you sing the lead tonight, something terrible will happen, something worse than you can imagine!

"We shall see!" said La Carlotta.

She decided this threat was the work of Christine. She thought Christine wanted to take over her part. La Carlotta called all her friends. She told them to come to the opera house and clap only for her, not for Christine.

A few hours later, La Carlotta received another note.

You have a bad cold. If you are wise, you will not sing tonight, or you will croak like a toad.

La Carlotta felt just fine. She ignored the note. She dressed and left for the opera house.

She would sing as planned.

CHAPTER 9

The Night of the Chandelier

That evening the opera began as usual. The hall was full. Mr. Moncharmin and Mr. Richard sat in Box Five.

The first act passed without a sign of the opera ghost.

"The ghost is late," Mr. Moncharmin said with a smile.

He and Mr. Richard shook hands and shared a good laugh.

In the second act, when La Carlotta appeared,

the audience clapped loudly and would not stop.

The managers left Box Five to see what all the fuss was about.

When they returned, they found a box of candy on the little shelf. They found a pair of opera glasses as well. Both men instantly remembered Mrs. Giry's story about the box of candy.

They looked at each other. Neither one felt like laughing. Then they became aware of a cold, strange draft. They sat down in silence.

Christine entered the stage and began to sing her small part. She saw Raoul in the audience. Her voice shook. She started to tremble.

With tears in his eyes, Raoul remembered the note he had received from Christine after they had each returned from the seaside town:

My Dearest,

You must have the courage not to see me again.
Do not speak of me again. If you love me, do this
for me. I will never forget you, my dear Raoul. My
life depends upon it. Your life depends upon it.

Christine

When Christine's song was over, no one clapped. Then, La Carlotta took the stage. The audience clapped very, very loudly.

La Carlotta's voice filled the room. Just then, a terrible thing happened. La Carlotta croaked like a toad, just as the opera ghost's note said she would!

The audience gasped.

Meanwhile, in Box Five, Mr. Moncharmin and Mr. Richard turned pale. La Carlotta's croak filled them with fear. Just then, they felt the ghost's breath. Mr. Moncharmin's hair stood on end.

The ghost was there: around them, behind them, beside them. They could feel him without seeing him. They heard his breathing. The men just stood there and trembled. They were afraid to run, afraid to stay.

On stage, La Carlotta opened her mouth to sing again. Once more, she croaked like a toad! The audience shuffled and whispered. They didn't know what to do.

"Well, go on!" Mr. Richard called down to La Carlotta from Box Five.

La Carlotta opened her mouth a third time, and out came another croak, then another, and another!

The audience went wild.

The two managers collapsed in their chairs. Suddenly, they heard a ghostly voice say, "She is singing to bring the chandelier down!"

Together Mr. Moncharmin and Mr. Richard

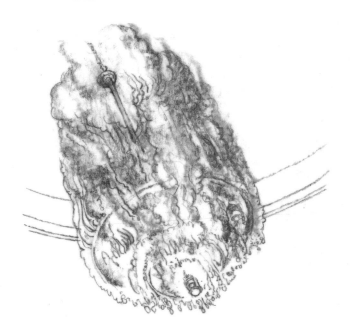

looked up at the ceiling. They screamed a terrible cry. The grand chandelier was slipping down. It was coming toward them!

The audience rushed for the doors as the chandelier plunged from the ceiling.

CHAPTER 10

Christine Disappears

～

That evening was tragic for everyone. La Carlotta fell ill, and Christine Daae disappeared.

Raoul was worried. Days later, he went to ask the new managers if they had seen Christine. They were still upset by the events of that night. They were working hard to repair the great chandelier. Someone had mysteriously cut the wires that held it in place. The managers did not have time to worry about Christine.

Raoul went to see Mrs. Valerius. She had cared for Christine her whole life, and Raoul thought that Christine would turn to her for help. When Raoul walked into Mrs. Valerius's apartment, he was surprised at how old and feeble she had become.

"Mrs. Valerius, have you seen Christine?" Raoul asked.

"She is with her Angel of Music," she told him. "Just as she always is."

Raoul dropped into a chair. He was very confused.

"Christine likes you very much," Mrs. Valerius told him in a low whisper. "She speaks of you every day. She told me you proposed to her," the old woman said. "But Christine can never marry," she said with sympathy.

"Is she engaged to someone else?" Raoul asked. His heart was breaking.

"She says the Angel of Music forbids her to marry," Mrs. Valerius replied. "If she marries, she will never hear him again. He has been teaching her at the opera house now for three months. He is a genius. Christine's voice is even more beautiful than it was before her lessons. She must not lose the Angel of Music. Surely you understand how important he is to her. He is the angel sent by her father, just as he promised."

"That was just a story for children," Raoul started to say.

"It is no story, sir. I have heard him sing," she added. "He has an angel's voice."

Raoul shook his head. He did not believe his ears.

"Tell me, Mrs. Valerius. Where does this angel live?" Raoul asked.

Mrs. Valerius looked at Raoul as if he were a fool. "At the opera house," she told him.

Raoul sprang from his chair. He left Mrs. Valerius's apartment in despair. Both the old woman and Christine believed in this angel, who would not let her marry. How would he ever be able to prove there was no angel at all?

Raoul thought a moment. He had heard rumors of a ghost who haunted the opera house, causing accidents and terrible things to happen. Was there a connection between the opera ghost and Christine's Angel of Music?

Raoul returned home to the house he shared with his brother, Count Philippe. Raoul was afraid that he might never be with Christine again.

"Forget about her, brother. Christine was seen last night, riding in a carriage. She was with someone, a shadowy outline of a man," Philippe said.

Raoul left quickly. He went to the spot where Christine's carriage had been seen. It was an icy, bitter night. Raoul stamped his feet to keep warm. He waited and watched, hoping Christine's carriage would drive by. At last, a carriage turned slowly onto the road. In the moonlight, Raoul saw Christine lean her head out the window.

"Christine!" Raoul called out.

In a flash, the carriage sped up and dashed past him. Raoul chased after it, but it was too late. The carriage was nothing more than a black spot on a white road. Christine had passed without even answering his call. Raoul stared down that cold, empty street into the pale, dead night. Nothing was colder than his heart.

The next morning Raoul received a note. It was from Christine. He opened it at once.

Dear Raoul,

Go to the masked ball at the opera tomorrow night. At twelve o'clock, be in the little room behind the chimney. Stand near the door that leads to the patio. Don't mention this appointment to any-one on Earth. Wear a white cloak and a mask. If you love me, do not let anyone recognize you.

Christine

CHAPTER 11

At the Masked Ball

∽

Raoul read the note over and over again. The envelope was covered in mud. It had been found outside the opera house. It looked as though it had been flung into the street with the hope that someone would pick it up and deliver it.

Raoul was now certain that Christine was a prisoner. Who was this Angel of Music?

Raoul bought a white cloak and a mask trimmed with long, thick lace. He was sure that no one would recognize him in this silly outfit. The masked ball had always been a noisy, crowded event, and Raoul thought that he would be unseen among the many people.

Decked out in his costume, Raoul arrived at the opera house at five minutes to twelve. He climbed the grand staircase, barely noticing the marble steps, or the rich setting. Raoul brushed past the other people wearing masks and costumes. He escaped from a mad whirl of dancers. Finally, he entered the small space that Christine had mentioned in her letter. The room was crammed with people.

Raoul leaned against the doorpost and waited. He did not stand there long. A figure in a black cloak passed by and squeezed his fingertips.

"Is that you, Christine?" he asked.

The figure in black raised her finger to her lips.

Raoul followed her in silence.

They passed a crowd gathered around a man dressed all in scarlet red. As Raoul walked by the

man, he recognized the face! It was the same face he had seen in the churchyard with Christine.

The figure in black grabbed Raoul's arm and dragged him away from the crowd. She hurried, checking behind her, as though she was being chased.

They went up two floors. The stairs and hallways were almost deserted. The black figure opened the door of a private box and slipped in. She invited Raoul to follow.

"Stay at the back of the box. Do not show yourself to anyone," Raoul heard Christine's voice whisper.

Christine put her ear to the wall and listened for a sound outside. She looked out into the hallway.

"He must have gone up higher," she started to say. "Wait! He is coming down again!"

Christine tried to close the door, but Raoul stopped her.

"I will speak with him!" Raoul declared. "He has no power over me!"

"No!" Christine cried out.

Raoul saw a red foot step toward the door. A second later, he was looking into a pair of scorched eyes.

"It is you! The one in the churchyard! This time you will not escape!" Raoul shouted at the figure.

Christine slammed the door.

"In the name of our love, Raoul, you shall not pass," she said

"You don't love me," Raoul cried. "You love that thing you have allowed to escape!"

Christine removed her mask. She was pale and sickly looking. There were deep lines around her eyes, and dark, sad shadows underneath them.

"One day you'll be sorry for your words, but I will forgive you," Christine said softly. "I came tonight to tell you good-bye."

Then Christine slipped out of the room and was gone.

Raoul searched the ball for her and for the figure in scarlet red. They were both gone.

Raoul went to Christine's dressing room. He tapped the door. There was no answer. He went in. The room was empty. Then he heard footsteps in the hallway. He hid behind the dressing-room curtain.

Christine entered her dressing room and flung her mask on the table.

Just then Raoul heard a faraway sound. Christine heard it, too. A faint singing came through the walls. The voice was very beautiful and soft. It was a heavenly voice. It came nearer and nearer. Soon the beautiful voice was in the room in front of Christine.

She rose and said, "Here I am. I am ready."

Raoul peeked out from behind the curtain. Who was Christine talking to? He saw no one but Christine. Yet the incredible voice kept on singing. He did not believe in ghosts or angels, but he had never heard anything so beautiful in his life. Raoul saw the blissful look on Christine's face. He saw her stretch out her arms to the voice.

The voice was real. Raoul was sure of it. He knew now that some mysterious and invisible master had put a spell on Christine. He had tricked her with his perfect voice into believing he was an angel.

In fact, he was nothing more than a pretender. Standing there behind the curtain, Raoul wondered, *Was this heavenly-sounding creature the mysterious opera ghost as well?*

Raoul had to fight against the music's charm. He stepped out from behind the curtain. He saw Christine walking toward the large mirror that hung on her dressing-room wall. Her arms were stretched toward her own reflection. She did not see Raoul.

He reached out to grab her, but a strange force flung him back. An icy blast swept over Raoul's face. Suddenly, he saw dozens of reflections of Christine spinning around him. Dizzy and confused, Raoul reached out his arms to grasp the real Christine, but he could not tell which one she was.

At last, everything stood still. Raoul saw only his own reflection. He could hardly understand what had happened.

Christine had disappeared into the mirror right before his eyes, just like a ghost.

CHAPTER 12

The Secret Engagement

ﻬ

The next day Raoul went again to ask Mrs. Valerius for help. To his surprise, Christine was there! Her cheeks were pink and rosy. Her eyes sparkled with a light from within. She wore a gold ring.

"What is this?" Raoul asked, taking her hand.

He didn't wait for her to speak but answered the question himself. "From the Angel of Music, no doubt! Christine, this angel is a fake and a liar. I cannot stand by and let you fall under his spell," Raoul said. "I was hiding in your dressing room last night. I heard his voice sing to you. I saw you disappear into the revolving mirror."

Christine gasped. "You must forget his voice. Forget what you saw. Forget everything about this mystery," she pleaded.

"Is it so very terrible?" Raoul asked.

"There is no more awful mystery on Earth," Christine replied. "You must promise never to come to my dressing room again, unless I send for you," she said.

"Meet me in the lobby of the opera house, then. Tomorrow," Raoul begged.

"Tomorrow," Christine agreed.

The next day Raoul went to the opera house. Christine met him in the lobby. She still wore the gold ring.

Together they roamed the many floors of the opera house. As they strolled, Raoul told her his plans. In a month, he was leaving France on an expedition to the North Pole. He wanted her to promise to marry him and come with him.

Christine shook her head, but the next instant an idea entered her mind. Her eyes lit up. She clapped her hands with glee.

"What are you thinking of, Christine?" Raoul asked.

"It is perfect. Your brother, Count Philippe, will never allow us to marry. Nor would the . . ." She stopped just before saying the word "angel."

"So for these few weeks, we will have a secret engagement," Christine whispered in excitement. "This is a happiness that will harm no one," she added.

Raoul hoped in his heart that Christine would come with him when it was time to leave. So he gave in to her secret plan for the moment. He hoped he might be able to find out the truth about this angel or ghost.

From that moment on, Raoul and Christine spent every day together.

Christine would not leave the opera house. She had to sing every night in La Carlotta's place, whose voice had not returned to normal.

Christine showed Raoul the backstage of the opera house. They explored all seventeen stories of the grand building. They ran along its frail bridges and they scrambled up and down forests of ropes. The happy days flew by.

Raoul did not ask Christine about the Angel of Music. But the ghost, or angel, was always in Raoul's thoughts.

One day, they passed by an open trapdoor in the floor. Raoul was curious. He looked down into the black hole and was about to step down when Christine dragged him away.

The trapdoor was slammed shut by an unseen hand.

"You must never go down there," Christine

said with a shiver. "Everything underground belongs to him."

From that day on, Christine became incredibly nervous. Her hands were ice-cold. Her eyes looked for imaginary shadows. She would laugh one moment and cry the next.

"Christine, what is it?" Raoul asked.

"Nothing!" Christine said.

"You must tell me the truth," Raoul insisted. "You are afraid of this place with its ghosts or angels. I can take you away from here, Christine. I promise you."

Christine paused.

"Is it possible?" she wondered aloud.

Christine grabbed Raoul's hand. She ran up a backstage ladder, dragging him behind her.

"Higher!" she cried.

Every few moments, Christine looked down past Raoul, afraid of what she might see.

They climbed through a maze of beams and

finally came to a stop on the rooftop of the opera house.

Despite her great care, Christine did not see that a shadow had been following them. It stopped when they stopped. It started when they started. It made no noise at all.

It watched and it listened as Christine told Raoul her story.

CHAPTER 13

Christine's Story

∽

On the roof, Christine breathed freely. It was a warm spring evening. The sun was setting. Clouds of gold and purple drifted slowly across the sky. Christine and Raoul could see all of Paris stretching out before them. Neither one of them noticed the shadow that had followed behind.

"I have only one day left," Christine told Raoul. "He has made me promise to live with him underground—forever!" Christine said.

"No one can force you to live underground!"

Raoul cried. "I will fight him to the death. I don't care if he is an angel, a ghost, or a man!"

"If I don't go with him, terrible things may happen! And he will come after me. He has put a spell on me with his singing. He cries those terrible tears from his two black eyeholes. I cannot bear the sight of those tears!" Christine sobbed.

Raoul held her close to his heart.

"So it is true. He is a man, and not an angel or a ghost as you and everyone else has always thought," Raoul said.

Christine nodded her head.

"He has a monster's face. He has had it since birth. He has an angel's voice, but a wounded animal's heart. And so, I made him a promise," Christine whispered.

"Let us go away, Christine. Let us go away at once!" Raoul said.

He tried to drag her away then and there.

Christine stopped him.

"No, not now. I have made my promise, and I must keep it," Christine said. "Let him hear me sing tomorrow evening. Perhaps if I sing for him one last time, he will understand our love and let me go. Then we can go away," she said.

A sigh sounded behind her.

Christine turned quickly.

"Did you hear that?" she asked fearfully.

"I heard nothing, my love," Raoul said. "Why does he have such power over you?"

"For three months I had heard him behind the mirror in my dressing room without seeing him. You have heard the voice, too. It is as beautiful as an angel's. Just like the angel my father promised to send me. My own voice sounded sweeter and more pure because of him.

"I was a fool to believe in an angel," Christine admitted. "He tricked me into following him to his home. He lives beneath the opera! We went down a dark passageway and walked through a hall. Then we came to a lake under the opera house! The darkness lifted only a bit and a blue light surrounded us.

"He covered his head with a hooded cloak so I could not see his face. We got into a little boat that was tied to a dock. He began to row across the lake toward the blue light. He told me his name is Erik," Christine whispered.

Christine looked into the shadows, afraid to go on.

"I was so scared, I must have fainted. I awoke in a drawing room filled with baskets of flowers. A man in a mask and a black cape stood in the room. When he spoke, I knew it was the voice! I was angry that he'd tricked me into coming to this place. I rushed at him and snatched the mask from his face!"

Christine put her head in her hands. "If I live to be a hundred, I will always hear Erik's horrible cry!" she said with a moan.

"It was a terrible sight. He has only black holes for his eyes, nose, and mouth."

" 'Now that you have torn off my mask, you can never leave!' he told me."

Christine trembled at the memory.

"How did you escape?" Raoul asked.

"I pretended he did not scare me. I listened to him play his music on a grand organ. He sobbed and begged me to love him. I felt sorry for him and promised to return. Erik believed me. Then he gave me this gold ring. He said as long as I wore it, *you* would be safe from harm."

"Does he control you with threats of harm to *me*?" asked Raoul.

Christine's eyes filled with tears at the thought. She nodded.

"My dearest, it is he who should be afraid of me," Raoul declared.

"You almost make me believe it is possible to escape," Christine said.

She laid her head on Raoul's shoulder. They sat in silence and gazed at the night sky. They still did not see the creeping black shadow of a cape. It came so near, it could have covered them both.

"You must come with me at once, Christine. Leave this nightmare behind you," Raoul declared.

At that moment, they heard a terrible, strangled cry beside them. Then an icy blast blew by.

"Run!" Christine cried.

Raoul followed her down the passageway from the rooftop. Suddenly the Foreign Stranger appeared as if out of thin air. This meant that the opera ghost could not be far behind. The Foreign Stranger pointed to another passage and shouted, "Go this way! Quickly!"

Christine and Raoul raced along hallways and down stairs to Christine's dressing room.

Christine looked down at her hand. The gold ring was gone!

"I've lost the ring!" she cried. "It must have slipped from my finger as we ran from the roof. He will be angry if he sees me without it. He'll think I've broken my promise to return!"

Christine pushed Raoul toward the exit door.

"Let us run away at once," Raoul demanded.

Christine waited a moment. She heard a noise in the hallway.

"No! Tomorrow. Meet me in my dressing room at exactly midnight. Erik will be waiting for me underground in his house on the lake. After I have sung for him, it will be safer for us to escape then," Christine insisted.

"At exactly midnight," Raoul repeated.

"Yes, now go!" Christine said.

She gave him a parting kiss.

CHAPTER 14

The Two Brothers Fight

The next morning when Raoul awoke, Count Philippe was waiting to speak with him.

"Read that!" Philippe said, handing Raoul a copy of the newspaper.

Raoul read about how he was engaged to be married to Christine.

Raoul put down the newspaper.

"I don't know how that got into the newspaper, brother. But it's true. I do intend to run away with Christine tonight!" Raoul announced.

"You must not do anything so foolish," Philippe said.

"It's too late, Philippe," Raoul said as he walked out of the room.

"I will stop you!" Philippe called after him.

Raoul spent the rest of the day preparing for his escape with Christine. He hired a new carriage and horses. He bought new luggage and supplies for the journey.

By nine o'clock that night, everything was ready.

Raoul parked his carriage behind the opera house. Two other carriages were parked there as well. One of them was Philippe's.

Raoul went into the opera house to hear Christine sing.

Outside, a shadow in a long black cape examined the two carriages carefully.

CHAPTER 15

Christine Disappears Again!

That night, Raoul sat in the audience. He did not sit with his brother, Philippe, in their usual box.

Christine sang with all her heart and soul. Her hair spilled over her shoulders. Her arms stretched out to her admirers. Her eyes turned to Raoul.

Suddenly, the stage went dark. Then, in a flash, the lights came back on. The stage was empty. Christine was gone!

Raoul uttered a cry. Count Philippe sprang to his feet.

"Where is she?" the audience cried.

Everyone spoke at once. Raoul hurried out of his seat. Count Philippe disappeared from his box. The audience grew restless and noisy.

At last, the conductor said in a sad and serious voice, "Ladies and Gentlemen, Christine Daae has disappeared before our very eyes. The performance is over!"

CHAPTER 16

The Managers Behave Strangely

Behind the stage there was a bustle of activity.

"Where is Christine?" someone asked.

"She's run away with that man Raoul," said someone else.

"No, it was the ghost!" another whispered.

"Where are the managers?" asked Mr. Mercier, the assistant manager.

"Locked in their office," answered Gabriel, the choirmaster.

"Where is the light-man?" asked Mr. Mercier. "Perhaps he can explain what happened."

"He and his two assistants are missing," answered Gabriel.

Gabriel and Mr. Mercier exchanged a worried look. They remembered that Joseph Buquet, the chief stagehand, had been missing, too, before his tragic accident. Just then a police detective arrived on the scene.

"I have sealed off all the exits above and below the opera house," the detective said. "Tell the managers I must speak with them."

The detective turned away to start the search for Christine.

"Go and get the managers, Gabriel," Mr. Mercier said.

"I have tried," Gabriel replied. "When I knocked on the door, they said they were not to be disturbed. When I knocked again, Mr. Moncharmin opened the door and asked me for a safety pin. I told him I had none, and he shut the door in my face."

"Is this some sort of joke?" Mr. Mercier asked.

"The managers have behaved strangely all evening, Sir," Gabriel said.

"What were they doing?" Mr. Mercier asked.

"They wouldn't allow anyone near them. They didn't want people to walk behind them. They said something about not letting anyone get close to their back pockets. And they walked backward all night—up the stairs all the way to their office, backward!" Gabriel said.

"I will go myself," Mr. Mercier said.

Mr. Mercier knocked and knocked on the office door. At last Mr. Moncharmin opened it.

"Someone has run away with Christine Daae!" Mr. Mercier said quickly.

Mr. Moncharmin put something in Mr. Mercier's hand and said, "Good job!"

He quickly shut the door.

Mr. Mercier looked down at the object in his hand. It was a safety pin!

CHAPTER 17

A Mysterious Foreign Stranger

Raoul knew that Erik had taken Christine away. Erik had tricked everyone into believing that he was the opera ghost. He had fooled Christine into thinking that he was an Angel of Music sent by her father. He had to be the one who had taken Christine down into the dark pit below the opera.

Raoul rushed onto the stage. He thought he could hear Christine's cries through the thin boards of the stage floor. Raoul wanted to go down into that pit of darkness, but every entrance had been closed off by the police.

"Christine! Christine!" Raoul shouted.

People pushed Raoul aside, laughing. They made fun of him.

Terrible thoughts flashed through Raoul's mind. Had Erik discovered their secret plan to escape? What would he do to Christine?

Bitter tears scorched Raoul's eyelids. His throat filled with sobs. Raoul stumbled into Christine's dressing room. Oh, why had she refused to leave earlier?

Raoul fumbled awkwardly at the great mirror on the wall where Christine had disappeared just a few weeks before. He pushed it and pressed it but the glass would not move. It opened only for Erik.

Raoul went to find the managers. He would insist that they let him enter the dark passages below the opera house.

Just as he was about to enter the managers'

office, a hand was laid on his shoulder. Raoul heard these words spoken in his ear:

"The opera ghost's secrets are none of your business!"

Raoul turned to see who would dare protect the monster.

Raoul saw a thin and bony face with jade-green eyes. Raoul recognized him at once. It was the Foreign Stranger, who roamed the opera halls, and who had helped Christine and Raoul escape from the shadow on the roof the day before.

The Foreign Stranger held his finger to his lips.

Before Raoul could speak, the mysterious stranger bowed and faded into the darkness.

CHAPTER 18

The Police Accuse Count Philippe

Raoul entered the managers' office.

"Where is Christine?" Raoul demanded to know.

The managers ignored him. They were too busy arguing with each other.

"If your pocket was pinned with the safety pin, how could the ghost take our twenty thousand francs?" asked Mr. Moncharmin.

"Are you accusing *me* of taking the francs?" roared Mr. Richard.

"What else can I believe?" Mr. Moncharmin shouted back.

At that moment, Mr. Mifroid, the police detective, entered the room.

"Is Christine Daae in here?' Mr. Mifroid asked the managers.

"Is she gone?" Mr. Moncharmin replied.

"That terrible monster has taken her! We must get her back!" Raoul interrupted.

"Who has taken her?" Mr. Mifroid asked Raoul.

"Call him what you will. The Angel of Music. The Opera Ghost. They are one and the same. His real name is Erik. He is the monster who lives beneath the opera house!" Raoul shouted.

Mr. Mifroid looked at Raoul. Then he looked over at Mr. Moncharmin and Mr. Richard.

"I see. Have the two of you ever seen or heard of an opera ghost?" Mr. Mifroid asked the managers.

"Just this evening he stole twenty thousand francs right out of my pocket. And my pocket was securely pinned!" Mr. Richard said angrily.

Mr. Mifroid looked around. He was sure that all three men were out of their minds.

"Well, a ghost who carries off an opera singer and twenty thousand francs on the same evening must have his hands full," Mr. Mifroid joked.

Raoul, Mr. Moncharmin, and Mr. Richard began to speak at once. Just then another detective entered the room. He whispered something to Mr. Mifroid. Mr. Mifroid turned to Raoul.

"Sir, I understand that you were planning on running away with Miss Daae tonight," he said.

"Yes, until that monster carried her off," Raoul answered.

"Perhaps it was your brother who took Miss Daae," Mr. Mifroid suggested. "Perhaps he did this to prevent you from keeping your engagement and making your escape."

"Impossible!" Raoul said.

"Are you sure, Sir?" Mr. Mifroid asked. "Your

brother's carriage was seen racing away right after Miss Daae disappeared."

Raoul thought for a moment. He remembered how just that morning his brother had said he would stop him from marrying Christine.

"Excuse me, Mr. Mifroid. That doesn't solve the mystery of our missing twenty thousand francs," Mr. Richard noted.

Mr. Richard and Mr. Moncharmin started to yell and accuse each other all over again. Raoul raced out of the managers' office, down a long, dark passageway. If Philippe had kidnapped Christine, Raoul would rescue her.

A figure blocked his way.

"Where are you going, sir?" asked a voice.

Raoul squinted in the dark at a pair of jade-green eyes.

"You again! Who are you?" Raoul asked.

"I am the only one who can help you," the Foreign Stranger replied.

CHAPTER 19

Through the Looking Glass

"I hope that you have not told Erik's secret," the Foreign Stranger whispered.

"Is he your friend?" Raoul asked angrily.

"Erik's secret is also Christine Daae's secret. To talk about one would bring harm to the other," the Foreign Stranger reminded him.

"I don't have time for games, Sir," Raoul said. "I must find Christine. My brother, Philippe, has carried her away."

"Christine Daae is here in the opera house," said the Foreign Stranger. "With Erik."

"How can you be sure?" Raoul asked.

"This was a public kidnapping. It is something Erik would do to prove how clever he is," the Foreign Stranger said. "But he would not take her far. The opera is the only place where he feels safe."

"You know him then?" asked Raoul. "Will you help me? Will you help Christine?"

"I will try. I will take you to them. That is the best I can do," the Foreign Stranger said.

Raoul grasped the man's hands in his. They were ice cold.

"Let's hurry! We must rescue her at once," Raoul shouted.

"Quiet," the Foreign Stranger whispered.

"Do you think he is near?" Raoul asked.

"He hears everything. He may be in this wall, in this ceiling. Or he may already be at the house on the underground lake," the Foreign Stranger said. "Come! Quietly!"

The two men tiptoed down long passageways that Raoul had never seen before. The Foreign Stranger led Raoul into Christine's dressing room through an unfamiliar doorway.

"Sir, we are about to face an enemy more terrible than you can imagine," the Foreign Stranger said. "You must be prepared for everything. Do you truly love Christine?"

"With all my heart," Raoul answered without hesitation.

"Let your love be your strength, then," the Foreign Stranger said.

The Foreign Stranger took off his dark jacket, and put it on backwards to cover his white shirt. He raised the collar of the jacket against his neck and told Raoul to do the same.

"We must make ourselves as invisible in the dark as possible," the Foreign Stranger urged.

He then turned to the wallpaper around the great mirror. He pressed his face against the pattern, searching for something. After what seemed like a very long time, the Foreign Stranger said, "Aha! I have it!"

He pushed his finger against a spot in the pattern of the wallpaper.

"In half a minute, Sir, we will be in!" the Foreign Stranger said in triumph.

"We will go through the mirror as Christine has done?" Raoul asked.

"You have seen her leave through the revolving mirror?" the Foreign Stranger asked with a frown, looking back at the mirror with concern.

"It should start to open—now," the Foreign Stranger said.

They waited and watched.

"It's not turning," Raoul said.

"Perhaps he has cut the cord. Perhaps he knew we would try this." The Foreign Stranger sighed.

"Why would these walls obey only him?" Raoul asked.

"Because he built them," the Foreign Stranger replied. "He escaped from my country and became a builder in this one. He built the opera house to be his secret hiding place. He committed many terrible crimes in my country."

"We must find another way in," Raoul said, panic rising in his voice.

"Tonight there is no other," the Foreign Stranger told him. "Look out!" he cried.

Suddenly, the mirror turned, like a revolving door. It swept Raoul and the Foreign Stranger into the deepest darkness.

CHAPTER 20

Into the Darkness

The revolving mirror completed its circle. The two men stood still, holding their breath.

The Foreign Stranger slipped to his knees to search for a lantern that he knew Erik kept hidden there. Moments later, he shone a light so that Raoul could see the floor, the walls, and the ceiling. They were all made of wood. There was a small square of light that shone up through a space where the wall and the floorboards were joined.

Suddenly, they heard a click.

The Foreign Stranger turned off his small lantern. He whispered to Raoul, "Follow me and do exactly as I do."

Raoul and the Foreign Stranger crawled to the small square of light. They slipped through the space and hung by their hands from the floor-boards. They dropped into the cellar below. The air was thick and dark. They crawled on their hands and knees. They passed three bodies that lay very still.

"Are they alive?" Raoul asked in a low voice.

"It's the light-man and his assistants. They are asleep. Erik must have given them a sleeping potion," the Foreign Stranger whispered.

Raoul shuddered.

"Silence now, and follow me," the Foreign Stranger told him. "There are five cellars under the opera house. We must climb down to the third cellar. That is where we'll find the entrance to the monster's home."

Down, down, down they crept. At last they reached the third cellar. It was lit by a faint light in the distance. A sudden loud noise forced them to stop in their tracks.

"It may be him! We must not be discovered," the Foreign Stranger said.

Quickly, he led Raoul down two staircases to the fifth cellar. It was the deepest and darkest point beneath the opera house. There, the Foreign Stranger breathed a sigh of relief.

"We may rest a minute," he said. "He will not follow us here."

No sooner had he finished speaking when an incredible face came into sight. It was a head of fire with no body attached! The flaming face tore through the darkness. It came straight at Raoul and the Foreign Stranger.

"What can this be?" the Foreign Stranger cried. "He never comes to this side of the building. He built the opera house on swampy, wet ground. Erik knew it would form an underground lake where he could build his own house and be safe from intruders. His house is on the other side completely. I have never seen anything like this head of fire before. Perhaps he has sent it to capture us! We must run!"

They fled down a long passage that was open before them. The flaming face came after them. No matter how far or fast they ran, it was always right behind. They looked back. Now, they could see the face clearly. The eyes were round and staring. The nose was a little crooked. The mouth was large with a hanging lower lip. It looked like a bright, red moon. How did it manage to glide through the darkness with nothing to support it?

Still the thing approached.

They heard a horrible scraping noise, like that of a thousand nails against a chalkboard. Raoul and the Foreign Stranger could run no farther. The flaming head was almost upon them.

Raoul and the Foreign Stranger flattened themselves against the wall. They didn't know what was going to happen next. A terrible noise surrounded them, thousands of little, living screeches! Just as the flaming head came up to them, they knew what the noise was. It made their hairs stand on end from horror.

"It's the rat catcher!" the Foreign Stranger hissed. "His fire attracts the rats. He walks the passageways to catch them and lead them outside to the river. I forgot all about him. Don't move!"

The shadow of the rat catcher brushed past them. Little four-legged bodies wriggled between their feet, then climbed up their legs! Try as they might, Raoul and the Foreign Stranger could not stay still. They pushed back against the waves of little legs and nails and claws and teeth.

All at once, the rats passed by them.

Raoul and the Foreign Stranger were able to

breathe again. Trembling, they watched as the rat catcher continued down the passage, followed by thousands of scratching rats.

"Will it take long to cross the lake? We must get to the monster's house quickly," Raoul asked.

"We cannot enter his house from the lake," the Foreign Stranger said. "He uses a trick to guard the lake. He sings his enchanting songs through a reed pipe under the water. People who enter the lake can't resist his song. They follow the sound underwater and drown."

"How can we rescue Christine?" Raoul asked.

"We must return to the third cellar," the Foreign Stranger said. "We will find our way through there."

Once again Raoul followed the Foreign Stranger through the dark, musty passages.

"This way!" directed the Foreign Stranger.

Again they had to crawl on their hands and knees. They came to a large board propped up against a thick stone wall. The Foreign Stranger stopped, listened, and pointed to the wall.

"The entrance to his house is behind one of those stones." He spoke so softly that Raoul could barely hear him.

With Raoul close on his heels, the Foreign Stranger slipped behind the board. He pressed heavily upon the wall. A stone gave way! There was a hole just wide enough to fit through.

"Take off your shoes," he told Raoul, while he took off his own.

They wriggled through the hole and dropped into the monster's house. The darkness was thick. The silence was heavy and terrible.

Raoul turned to look back at the hole in the wall. It was gone! The stone had closed up by itself. There was no way out.

CHAPTER 21

The Room of Mirrors

⌒

The Foreign Stranger lit his small lantern. He moved the light over the center of the room. He noticed something very strange.

It was the trunk of a tree. Its leaves and branches ran right up the walls and disappeared into the ceiling. The tree seemed alive. But it was not. It was made of iron and it was cold to the touch.

Raoul passed his hand along each of the six walls. They were smooth as glass, and he saw the dark reflection of his shadow in every one.

"It is a room of mirrors!" Raoul exclaimed. "Is there a trapdoor or a spring, like the revolving mirror in Christine's dressing room?" Raoul asked.

"It is possible there is a spring, but it will be very difficult to find," the Foreign Stranger said unhappily.

He wiped the beads of sweat from his forehead.

"It is unfortunate for us that I've led us here," he told Raoul. "I had seen Erik come through the hole, but I'd never followed him through it before. I have heard of prison rooms like this one, but I've never been in one."

"What do you mean? Why do you speak in puzzles? We are wasting time. Take me to Christine, as you promised," Raoul ordered.

The Foreign Stranger put his hand on Raoul's shoulder to steady him.

"It is time I explained to you what I know of the monster," the Foreign Stranger said. "You must understand. I may have already done all that I can."

Raoul would not believe him.

"I must reach Christine," Raoul vowed.

He tried to climb the walls, but they were too smooth. He leaped upon the iron tree, but he could not crawl past the ceiling. He pushed against the stone that had opened up to allow them to drop in. This time it would not move.

Feeling defeated, Raoul slumped in the corner with his head in his hands.

The Foreign Stranger sat down across from Raoul and spoke softly.

"Erik looks like a monster, it is true. His horrible and deformed face made it difficult even for his parents to love him. All he ever wanted was to be loved. No one in the world has ever been able to look past his mask and see into his heart. As a result, he doesn't know how to love. At times he is like a naughty child. And when he is hurt, he can be very cruel," the Foreign Stranger said with a shudder.

"How do you know so much about him?" Raoul asked.

"I followed Erik from my country to yours," the Foreign Stranger said. "At one time he was a famous magician in the Middle East—the part of the world where I come from. I was the chief of police to the king of my country when Erik became a favorite of the princess. He amused her with his magic.

"He was also a great builder, and he made a special palace for my king to hide his royal treasure. After the palace was built, my king ordered Erik's death. The king wanted to make sure that Erik never told anyone about the secret hiding place he had built for him. I was the one who saved his life and helped him escape."

"You and Christine both pity this creature. I have seen it in your eyes," Raoul said. "Why?"

"Erik's own mother would turn her head away and make him wear a mask. She never once kissed him, or held him close.

"Erik has been treated badly by this world. You ask me why I pity him. I ask you, how can I not?"

The Foreign Stranger paused briefly and then continued. "When Erik escaped, the king blamed me. The king allowed me to leave my country, so long as I never returned. I followed Erik. I felt responsible for him. I was afraid that he might come to harm. I worried that if he was misunderstood, he might do harm as well.

"So for many years, I've watched over him at the opera house. I am his only friend. But Erik does not know how to be a friend. He does not know how to love, but he is starved for both friendship and love. Then one day he told me that he had fallen in love. He said he had found someone who loved him for himself."

"He has taken Christine from me by force. I have no pity for him," Raoul replied.

"I would have done anything to prevent him from hurting you and Christine. When he took her away the first time, I tried to rescue her. I crossed the lake to his house. Erik almost drowned me, until he realized who I was.

"While you two played at your secret engagement, I kept watch over you. I did what I could, but it wasn't enough," the Foreign Stranger added with a sad shake of his head.

Suddenly they heard a noise through the wall.

CHAPTER 22

Trapped!

Raoul scrambled to his feet. The Foreign Stranger put a finger to his lips to warn him to be silent.

From the other side of the wall, they heard a door open and shut. They heard a dull moan.

Then they heard Erik's voice. "You must make your choice— a wedding song or a funeral song. The wedding song is happy. The funeral song is . . . not. Which will it be?"

There was another moan, then a long silence.

Raoul jumped up, ready to break through any one of the six mirrored walls. But the Foreign Stranger grabbed him.

"He does not know we are here. We must keep it that way," the Foreign Stranger whispered.

"Look!" they heard Erik say. "I have invented a mask that makes me look like anybody else. People will not even turn around when they see me. You and I can go out together in the world above, like other loving couples. You will be the happiest of women. We will sing, all by ourselves—"

Erik stopped in the middle of his sentence.

"You are crying! You are afraid of me! Why? I am not really so wicked. All I ever wanted was to be loved for myself. If you loved me, I should be as gentle as a lamb," Erik said.

His voice grew louder and more despairing. "You don't love me! You don't love me!" he cried.

Then there was silence.

Raoul and the Foreign Stranger waited, afraid to breathe.

Their only chance of escape was to let Christine know they were there. Only she could open the door on the other side of the wall.

They hoped that Erik had, at last, left Christine alone behind the wall. Suddenly the silence was broken by the ringing of a bell.

"Ah, someone has entered the lake, I see." Erik said. "I will have to greet my new visitor with a special song," he added with an evil chuckle.

Raoul heard footsteps moving away and a door opening and closing. There was no time to waste. Christine was finally alone behind the wall!

"Christine! Christine!" Raoul called.

There was no reply.

Raoul called out again many times, until at last they heard a soft voice say, "I am dreaming!"

"Christine. It's me, Raoul. It is not a dream. If you are alone, you must answer me!" Raoul cried. "We have come to save you. When you hear Erik returning, warn us!"

Christine began to tremble, afraid that Erik would discover where Raoul was hidden.

In a few hurried words she said, "If I don't agree to be his wife, he will kill everybody. I have until eleven o'clock tomorrow evening. Then I must choose, or everybody in the opera house will be dead and buried," she sobbed.

"Where is Erik now?" the Foreign Stranger asked.

Christine replied that he must have left the house.

"Can you make sure?" the Foreign Stranger asked.

"I am tied up tightly. I cannot move at all," she said. "Where are you?"

"In the room of mirrors," Raoul told her.

"The door to that room is locked on this side. Erik has forbidden me ever to enter it," Christine said, despair filling her voice.

"Do you know where the key is?" Raoul asked.

"The key is in the next room," Christine cried out. "Raoul, you must leave! Go back the way you came!"

"Christine," said Raoul, "I will leave here only if we go together!"

"Miss," the Foreign Stranger interrupted them. "Erik will untie you. You have only to pretend to play along! Remember that he loves you! Smile at him. Charm him with your eyes. Tell him that the ties hurt, and that you will not run away."

"Hush! I hear something," Christine whispered. "He's back!"

Heavy steps sounded slowly behind the wall. Next there came a cry of pain from Christine.

"Why do you cry out?" the men heard Erik ask.

"Loosen these ties, I beg you," Christine answered.

Erik did as Christine asked.

He then started pacing about the room. He was dripping wet. Erik sat down at the grand organ and began to play a sad funeral song.

"In memory of the fellow I met in the lake. He should not have come looking for me. He will never come looking for me or anyone else again," Erik muttered to himself.

Then he began to sing. His voice thundered through the air like a raging storm. He took no notice of Christine.

Christine crept into the other room. She grabbed the forbidden key and returned with it, just as the grand organ came to a crashing halt.

Erik's voice cut through the air.

"What are you doing, Christine?"

CHAPTER 23

The Intruders Are Discovered!

❦

Christine ran to unlock the door to Raoul and the Foreign Stranger's prison.

"What is this room that you've never let me see? I am curious!" Christine told Erik, trying to sound playful.

"I don't like curious people," Erik said. "Give me the key. Now!" he commanded.

Erik took the key from her by force. Christine cried out in pain.

Raoul couldn't help himself. He shouted a cry of rage.

"What was that?" Erik asked.

"I heard nothing!" Christine replied.

"I heard a cry!" Erik insisted.

"I cried out because you hurt me," Christine said. "I heard nothing else."

"You're lying," Erik said. "Why do you stand by the door like that?"

Erik paused a moment.

"There's someone in the Room of Mirrors! I understand everything now!" Erik snarled.

"There is no one!" Christine cried out.

"Well, it won't take long to find out," Erik said with a nasty chuckle.

All of a sudden the Room of Mirrors was flooded with a hot, bright white light. Surprised, Raoul staggered back against the wall with a *thump.*

"Aha! I told you there was someone!" the monster's voice roared. "There's a tiny peephole at the top of the wall. Go. Tell me what you see!"

Raoul and the Foreign Stranger heard steps being dragged against the wall. They could hear Christine say, "There is no one in there."

"No one? Are you sure?" Erik asked.

Christine peeped in through the tiny hole. For a moment, she was relieved to see that Raoul and the Foreign Stranger were unharmed.

"Turn out the light, Erik. No one is in there," Christine assured him.

"Well, then, let me show you one of my little tricks —to pass the time, shall I?" Erik asked in an evil tone.

Erik began to sing in a high-pitched tone. His voice was everywhere. It pierced the air. It echoed and boomed against the mirrored walls. Raoul and the Foreign Stranger covered their ears against the loud, sharp notes.

At the same time, the hot, white light in the Room of Mirrors grew even brighter.

"Erik, why is the wall to this room so hot?"

Christine asked in a worried voice. She pulled her hand away from the heat of the wall.

"Unbearable, isn't it?" Erik answered. "It's one of my favorite inventions. I can heat up a room to a terrible temperature, just by turning on a bright, white heat light."

"Erik, make it stop!" Christine called out.

"Those who nose around my Room of Mirrors are doomed to die of thirst and heat, as if they were lost in the great tropical forests of Africa!" Erik said, laughing.

"Forests of Africa? What does that mean?" Christine cried out. "Stop this, Erik! Stop it!"

Raoul tried to hear Christine, but all he could hear was Erik's never-ending laughter.

Then he heard the sound of a body falling on the floor. Raoul heard a noise of something dragging, a door slam, and then . . . nothing.

CHAPTER 24

Room of Mirrors, Room of Illusions

☙

Raoul hammered his fists against the hot, thick mirrored walls. His hands burned and the walls would not break. He looked for something to throw at the mirrors, but the room had no furniture. There was no way of breaking free. The light from the ceiling grew brighter. The temperature of the walls and the floor kept rising.

In the white-hot light, the iron tree and its branches appeared to multiply in the mirrored walls into hundreds of trees. The ceiling light looked just like a hot tropical sun. In the awful

heat, Raoul began to believe that they really were trapped under the hot, blazing sun in an African forest. Erik's trick was working.

"It is an invention of the mind, an illusion Erik is creating with the mirrors and the lights," the Foreign Stranger explained.

Raoul would not listen. He was convinced that they were really in Africa. He shouted for help, pacing restlessly up and down the room. The Foreign Stranger tried to calm him.

"We are in a room, a little room. That is what you must keep saying to yourself. There must be a trick, a spring, or a button that will open the door. We will leave the room as soon as I discover it," the Foreign Stranger said in a soothing voice.

Raoul lay flat on the ground. The Foreign Stranger feared for Raoul's mind and hunted for the spring that would open the door. He fumbled and pressed against every inch of the mirrored glass wall. He found absolutely nothing.

In the next room, all was silent.

Meanwhile, a confused Raoul searched for Christine among the trees. He thought he saw her hiding and called out to her. His sadness brought tears to the Foreign Stranger's eyes.

"How thirsty I am!" Raoul cried out in his madness.

The Foreign Stranger was also thirsty, yet he kept on hunting for a way out. He knew that "night" in this make-believe forest would be worse than daytime.

It was.

CHAPTER 25

Out of the Forest and Into the Desert

༽

The Foreign Stranger struggled to remember that this was all an illusion. But he couldn't help slipping in and out of the nightmare that Erik had created.

When Erik turned out the light, the heat in the room did not stop. In fact, it became even hotter in the dark. Both men were drenched in sweat.

Suddenly, Raoul and the Foreign Stranger heard a lion roar a few yards away.

"Oh, he is quite close! In that bush, over there!" cried Raoul.

The lion roared again and again.

Raoul pounded his fists against the wall. He smashed the mirror, but made no dent in the wall behind it. The Foreign Stranger tried to stop him.

"There is no lion," he explained. "It is Erik in the next room, roaring through a tube."

Raoul would not listen.

Tired from all his efforts, the Foreign Stranger threw himself on the floor and went to sleep. He told Raoul it would be wise for him to do the same.

The next morning, the African forest was gone. In its place, Erik had created the illusion of an immense desert of sand, stones, and rocks.

Raoul's thirst was so great he could barely speak above a whisper.

"Erik! Stop it! Please!" the Foreign Stranger shouted, as loudly as he could.

There was no answer. Instead, all around them lay the silence of that bare, stony desert.

Raoul raised himself on his elbow. He pointed to a spot on the horizon. He had discovered an oasis!

The Foreign Stranger recognized it at once. It was the worst of the illusions. No one had ever been able to fight against it—the hope for water.

"No, don't believe in the water. It's another trick of Erik's mirrors," the Foreign Stranger shouted.

But Raoul ignored him. He dragged himself along, crying for water, his mouth open.

Then suddenly, they not only saw water, they heard it! They heard water flow and ripple before them. Then they heard the sound of rain, but it was not raining!

Erik was holding a long, narrow box filled with little stones. He shook it and the stones bounced, making a pattering noise that sounded exactly like rain.

Raoul and the Foreign Stranger were so thirsty they started licking the mirror. They couldn't help themselves. It was burning hot! The two roared in pain and rolled on the floor.

That's when the Foreign Stranger saw it: a black nail in the wall. At last he had discovered the spring!

He pressed the nail. The nail moved but the door in the wall did not. A flap in the floor opened up instead. Cool air came up to them from the black hole below. In the dim light they saw a staircase.

Without hesitation, Raoul and the Foreign Stranger crawled down the stairs.

The winding staircase led them into darkness. They could almost taste the water in the cool air. The lake could not be far away.

They soon reached the bottom of the stairs. Their eyes could now see in the dark. They saw many circular shapes around them.

Raoul and the Foreign Stranger were surrounded by barrels! They were in Erik's cellar.

"This must be where he keeps his water," the Foreign Stranger said with a happy cry. "There will be plenty to drink here!"

The barrels were lined up in two rows, one on either side of the two men. All the barrels were sealed shut. There didn't seem to be any way to open them to drink.

Raoul grabbed a barrel and brought his pocket-knife down hard on it. The barrel split open. Raoul dipped his hand inside.

There was no water in the barrels. There was only gunpowder. There were enough barrels of gunpowder to blow up the entire opera house.

Now they knew the monster's evil plan.

CHAPTER 26

The Grasshopper or the Scorpion?

Christine had until eleven o'clock in the evening to make her decision. If she told Erik that she would not marry him, was it possible that he would really blow up the opera house?

All Erik had to do was set a spark to the gunpowder barrels. Everyone in the opera house would be buried under the ruins. Erik had chosen his time well, since there would be many people in the opera house. It would be the middle of a show.

"What time is it?" the Foreign Stranger asked Raoul.

Raoul could not see his watch in the dark.

Quickly they dragged themselves through the darkness. They felt their way back up the stone steps. They searched for the trapdoor to the Room of Mirrors.

At last they found it. They tumbled into the Room of Mirrors. It was as dark as the cellar.

The Foreign Stranger called out through the walls. "Erik! Erik! You cannot do this. Don't you remember? I saved your life!"

No one answered.

Raoul broke the glass that covered the face of his watch. His fingertips felt the position of the two watch hands.

"It is almost eleven o'clock now," Raoul said in a voice filled with fear.

Just then they heard footsteps in the next room. Someone tapped against the wall.

Christine called out, "Raoul! Raoul!"

All three spoke at once through the wall. Christine sobbed with relief to know that Raoul was still alive.

For hours she had promised Erik that if he would take her to the Room of Mirrors, she would say yes and marry him. He raved at her but would not do as she asked.

"He is quite mad!" Christine told them. "He showed me two bronze figures attached to the wall, a scorpion and a grasshopper. He said if I turned the scorpion around, that would mean 'yes' to marrying him. The grasshopper would mean 'no.' He told me I had only five minutes to decide."

"What time is it, Christine?" Raoul asked.

"It is almost five minutes to eleven," Christine replied, crying.

"What did he say next, Miss?" the Foreign Stranger asked in a low voice. "It is very important you tell us everything."

"His last words were, 'Be careful of the grass-hopper. It hops very high!'" Christine said.

"The grasshopper must be a switch that will blow up the gunpowder barrels in the cellar!" the Foreign Stranger told them.

"Turn the scorpion, Christine!" Raoul shouted through the wall.

"No, wait!" the Foreign Stranger said. "It has been much longer than five minutes. It may be a trick. The scorpion may be the switch!"

"Here he comes!" Christine cried out. "I hear him! Here he is!"

Raoul and the Foreign Stranger heard Erik's steps through the wall.

"Erik! It's me! Don't you remember?" the Foreign Stranger called to him.

"So, you are still alive in there?" Erik asked calmly.

The Foreign Stranger tried to speak again.

"Silence! Or I will blow everything up!" Erik said in a cold, dead voice.

Then he turned to Christine.

"The choice is up to you. If you turn the grasshopper, we will all be blown up, along with a whole quarter of Paris. If you turn the scorpion, to celebrate our wedding, all the gunpowder will be soaked and drowned. Only you can save the people of Paris. And then we can be happily married!" Erik said with a terrible laugh.

"Do you promise me that the scorpion is the one to turn?" Christine asked.

"Yes," Erik smiled.

Christine paused.

"Ah, so you won't have me? Then I will turn the grasshopper!" Erik said.

"No!" Christine said. "Erik! Look! I have turned the scorpion!"

CHAPTER 27

The Monster's Trick

⁓

Raoul and the Foreign Stranger dropped to their knees, expecting the worst. When there was no explosion, they breathed a sigh of relief.

Then they felt something crack beneath their feet. A terrible hissing sound filtered through the open trapdoor.

The noise came softly at first, then louder, and then very loudly. It was not the hiss of fire. It was the hiss of water! Then it became a gurgling sound.

Raoul and the Foreign Stranger rushed to the

trapdoor. The water rose up from the cellar. They drank and drank till they were no longer thirsty.

"Erik! Turn off the water!" the Foreign Stranger called out.

"Christine!" Raoul shouted. "The water is up to our knees!"

Christine was no longer there. They heard nothing but the water rising.

It came up to their chins and then to their mouths. They slipped. Water spun them around, smashing them into the dark mirrors. They climbed up the iron tree and clung to its branches.

The water rose still higher.

They choked as they struggled against the black water. They could hardly breathe what little air was left above the surface.

They lost their strength. The iron tree slipped from their groping fingers. They started sinking into the water. Then everything went dark.

CHAPTER 28

The Foreign Stranger Survives

∽

It was Christine who saved the Foreign Stranger from near death.

How do I, the author, know this? I learned it from the Foreign Stranger himself. I went to see him, not too long ago. He was very ill. His poor face looked very worn. His memory, however, was quite clear. This is what the Foreign Stranger told me about that awful night.

The last thing he remembered was the water rising above his head. Then everything went black. When he opened his eyes, he saw that he was lying on a bed. Raoul was lying on a sofa along the wall. Christine stood in the corner.

Beside her was a chest of drawers, wooden chairs, a clock on the mantel, red pin cushions, lacy pillows, and a few lamps. The Foreign Stranger was surprised to find such a normal-looking room in the cellar of the opera.

Erik, in his mask and cape, bent over him.

"Do you like my furniture?" he asked. "It is all that I have left from my mother."

Christine did not say a word. She moved silently and brought Erik a cup of tea. He gave it to the Foreign Stranger. Raoul had not moved. The Foreign Stranger looked with concern at Raoul's still body.

"Raoul is quite well," Erik told the Foreign Stranger. "He is merely . . . asleep. We must not wake him."

Erik left the room for a moment. The Foreign Stranger called to Christine. She sat gazing into the fire and did not answer him. Erik returned and said, "You are now saved. Soon I will take you up to the surface, as my wife has asked me to. But do not speak to my wife again. It might be very dangerous to your health."

The Foreign Stranger fell back asleep. When he woke next, he was propped up against his apartment door. He had been left there by someone.

As soon as he recovered, the Foreign Stranger asked people about Raoul. He learned that the young man had not been seen since the night that Christine disappeared. He also learned that Raoul's brother's body had been found on the bank of the opera lake. Philippe was the one who had drowned in the lake the night of Christine's failed rescue. The Foreign Stranger hung his head in sorrow. He had not been able to save Philippe or Raoul or Christine.

Erik's old friend went straight to the police. He wanted to tell them everything he knew. But the police did not want to hear his story.

By this time, the opera managers had shut down the opera and moved away. The police had better things to do than to look for an opera ghost. They did not believe in ghosts and had no use for anyone who did. Once the opera house was shut down, the police simply closed the case on all the strange events that had taken place. And that was the end of that.

The Foreign Stranger decided to write a story for the newspaper about all that had happened at the opera house. It took him weeks to write the tale. He wanted to get every detail just right.

One night, when he had just finished working on the story, there was a sharp knock at the door. The Foreign Stranger opened the door. He gasped as though he'd seen a ghost. There stood Erik!

CHAPTER 29

The Ghost's Love Story Ends

∽

Erik looked extremely weak. His forehead was white as wax. The rest of his horrible face was hidden by his mask.

"Murderer! You killed Count Philippe. What have you done with Raoul and Christine?" the Foreign Stranger asked.

Erik jumped back from this attack. He was silent a moment. Then he dragged himself to a chair.

"Count Philippe was an accident. His drowning

was an accident! I didn't mean to do it . . ." Erik started to say.

"You lie!" the Foreign Stranger shouted.

Erik bowed his head and said, "I have come here to tell you that I am going . . . to die."

"Where are Raoul and Christine?" the Foreign Stranger demanded to know.

"I am dying," Erik repeated.

"Raoul and Christine!" the Foreign Stranger demanded again. "Tell me if they are alive or dead!"

Erik paused a moment. "Christine is not dead," he told him. "She begged me to save you and Raoul. I would have left you both to drown. Christine came to me and promised she would stay underground and love me forever, if only I would spare the two of you."

"What have you done with Raoul?" the Foreign Stranger asked again.

Erik paused and hung his head.

"I couldn't allow him to leave," Erik explained. "He would have come after me, after Christine. He would never have left us alone so we could be happy. I locked him up in the deepest, darkest part of the opera house. I had to do it.

"When I returned, Christine was waiting for me as she had promised. I tore off my mask. She did not run away. Then, she kissed me on the cheek and said, 'Poor Erik!' At that moment, I felt all the happiness in the world!" Erik sobbed.

"I gave her the plain gold wedding band she'd lost," Erik continued. "I slipped it into her hand and told her, 'Take it for you and Raoul! It will be my wedding present to you both.'

"She asked me in a soft voice why I was letting her go. How could I explain it? Christine was the only one who had ever shown me kindness. She didn't run when she saw my horrible face. She had looked past my mask and into my heart.

She deserved to be happy and free. But without her, I can never be either," Erik said, his voice full of sadness.

Erik asked the Foreign Stranger to look away. He was choking and had to take off his mask. The Foreign Stranger got up and stood with his back turned, staring out a window. Suddenly, his heart was full of pity for Erik. After a lifetime of cruel treatment, a drop of kindness had shown Erik how to be kind in return.

"I freed Raoul from the room where I'd locked him up," Erik continued, "and told him to come with me to Christine. I asked her to promise me to come back for one reason: to bury me with the gold ring I had given her, which she was to wear until the moment I was buried. I told her where she would find me. Then she reached over, and she kissed me again, right here on the forehead.

"Raoul and Christine went off together, and I

was left to cry all alone. But I know Christine will keep her promise. She will come back to me soon," Erik said, putting his mask back on.

"Where have they gone?" asked the Foreign Stranger.

"Far away," said Erik sadly. "Where they could be happy."

"I am trusting you to let Christine know of my death. Please put a notice in the newspaper. Christine will know what to do," Erik added.

That was all.

Erik put his mask back on. The Foreign Stranger turned around and went with Erik to the door, watching him step into a cab. From the doorway, the Foreign Stranger heard Erik say, "Take me to the opera."

The cab drove off into the night.

The Foreign Stranger never saw Erik again. Three weeks later, a notice was published in the newspaper, which said, simply: ERIK IS DEAD.

CHAPTER 30

The Author Explains All Things

I have now told the unusual but true story of the opera ghost.

Although it has been many years since these events have taken place, the mysteries of the opera house have always haunted me. I felt it was my responsibility to find out the truth.

I uncovered many of the secret passages that Raoul and the Foreign Stranger had used to get to the cellars. I found the darkest, deepest place in the opera house where Erik had kept Raoul for countless days. On its walls were carved the letters "R" and "C," for Raoul and Christine.

I could not find Erik's house on the lake. Before his death, Erik blocked all the passages that led to it. As for his tricks, I discovered the key to almost all of them.

How did Erik appear and disappear from Box Five? The marble column beside the box appears quite solid. However, it is hollow, so someone can hide inside of it. Erik was able to speak to anyone in the box from inside the column and never be seen.

How did Erik take the twenty thousand francs from Mr. Richard's safety-pinned pocket? Erik had installed all the trapdoors in the opera house. He knew where each and every trapdoor led. He came up through one that was in the managers' office. It was narrow, just large enough for him to squeeze his arm through. He easily took the money from Mr. Richard's pocket while the coat hung over his chair.

But once Erik gave up his plan to marry Christine, he gave up everything, including money. Erik used the same trapdoor to return the money back to Mr. Richard's jacket pocket.

I learned that Erik grew up in a small French town. He was born with a terrible wasting disease that ate away at his face and hands, exposing the skeleton beneath the ragged skin. He ran away at an early age from his father's house.

The only way he could earn a living was by working at fairs, where he was paid to put his ugliness on display. He learned to be an artist and a magician at the fairs. His hideous face and heavenly voice were soon known far and wide.

Escaping from a king who wanted him dead, Erik came to Paris and dreamed of becoming a famous builder. He wanted to be just like everyone else. He put the magic and his music behind him.

He set about constructing the opera house—with all the amazing skill that he had used to build the king's palace in his homeland.

In the cellars of the opera house, his artistic nature took over again. He wanted to create a home that would be unseen and unknown by the rest of the world. There, he could hide from men's eyes forever.

Poor, unhappy Erik! With an ordinary face, he would have been considered a talented and famous genius. In the end, he had to be satisfied with the cellar of the opera.

We should, indeed, pity this poor creature. I was there when they removed his skeleton from the opera house. I saw the plain gold ring on his bony finger. Christine had slipped it on his hand when she came to bury him.

Christine had kept her promise.

What Do *You* Think?
Questions for Discussion

ᕙᕗ

Have you ever been around a toddler who keeps asking the question "Why?" Does your teacher call on you in class with questions from your homework? Do your parents ask you questions about your day at the dinner table? We are always surrounded by questions that need a specific response. But is it possible to have a question with no right answer?

The following questions are about the book you just read. But this is not a quiz! They are designed to help you look at the people, places, and events in the story from different angles. These questions do not have specific answers. Instead, they might make you think of the story in a completely new way.

Think carefully about each question and enjoy discovering more about this classic story.

1. Meg tells Joseph Buquet not to speak of the opera ghost or else he will have bad luck. Is she right? Do you believe in bad luck?

2. Why does Christine tell Raoul that she doesn't remember him? Have you ever lied to someone? Why did you do it?

3. Why do the new managers think the opera ghost is a joke? Do you believe in ghosts?

4. What happens when the seats are sold in Box Five? Do you think the opera ghost is right to be angry that his seat was sold? Has anyone ever taken something that you thought was yours?

5. Why does Christine so blindly follow the

Angel of Music? Do you think the gifts he gives her are worth the sacrifices she must make?

6. Christine's note to Raoul tells him to have courage enough to never see her again. What is the most courageous thing you've ever done?

7. Which option does Christine choose: the grasshopper or the scorpion? Do you think she makes the right decision? What is the most difficult choice you have ever had to make?

8. The Foreign stranger asks Raoul how he could do anything but pity Erik. Do you think Erik deserves Raoul's pity?

9. How does the opera ghost manage his "hauntings"? How did you feel to learn that it was all a trick?

10. Erik says of Christine, "I tore off my mask. She did not run away. . . . At that moment, I felt all the happiness in the world." Why do you suppose this makes him so happy?

Afterword
by Arthur Pober, Ed.D.

❧

First impressions are important.

Whether we are meeting new people, going to new places, or picking up a book unknown to us, first impressions count for a lot. They can lead to warm, lasting memories or can make us shy away from any future encounters.

Can you recall your own first impressions and earliest memories of reading the classics?

Do you remember wading through pages and pages of text to prepare for an exam? Or were you the child who hid under the blanket to read with a flashlight, joining forces with Robin Hood to save Maid Marian? Do you remember only how long it took you to read a lengthy novel such as *Little Women*? Or did you become best friends with the March sisters?

Even for a gifted young reader, getting through long chapters with dense language can easily become overwhelming and can obscure the richness of the story and its characters. Reading an abridged, newly crafted version of a classic novel can be the gentle introduction a child needs to explore the characters and story-line without the frustration of difficult vocabulary and complex themes.

Reading an abridged version of a classic novel gives the young reader a sense of independence and the satisfaction of finishing a "grown-up" book. And when a child is engaged with and inspired by a classic story, the tone is set for further exploration of the story's themes, characters, history, and details. As a child's reading skills advance, the desire to tackle the original, unabridged version of the story will naturally emerge.

If made accessible to young readers, these stories can become invaluable tools for understanding themselves in the context of their families and social environments. This is why the Classic Starts series includes questions that stimulate discussion regarding the impact and social relevance of the characters and stories today. These questions can foster lively conversations between children and their parents or teachers. When we look at the issues, values, and standards of past times in terms of how we live now, we can appreciate literature's classic tales in a very personal and engaging way.

Share your love of reading the classics with a young child, and introduce an imaginary world real enough to last a lifetime.

Dr. Arthur Pober, Ed.D.

Dr. Arthur Pober has spent more than twenty years in the fields of early childhood and gifted education. He is the former principal of one of the world's oldest laboratory schools for gifted youngsters, Hunter College Elementary School, and former Director of Magnet Schools for the Gifted and Talented for more than 25,000 youngsters in New York City.

Dr. Pober is a recognized authority in the areas of media and child protection and is currently the U.S. representative to the European Institute for the Media and European Advertising Standards Alliance.

Explore these wonderful stories in our
Classic Starts™ library.

20,000 Leagues Under the Sea

The Adventures of Huckleberry Finn

The Adventures of Robin Hood

The Adventures of Sherlock Holmes

The Adventures of Tom Sawyer

Anne of Green Gables

Arabian Nights

Around the World in 80 Days

Black Beauty

The Call of the Wild

Dracula

Frankenstein

Gulliver's Travels

Heidi

The Hunchback of Notre-Dame

The Jungle Book

The Last of the Mohicans

Little Lord Fauntleroy

A Little Princess

Little Women

The Man in the Iron Mask

Oliver Twist

The Phantom of the Opera

Pinocchio

Pollyanna

The Prince and the Pauper

Rebecca of Sunnybrook Farm

The Red Badge of Courage

Robinson Crusoe

The Secret Garden

The Story of King Arthur and His Knights

The Strange Case of Dr. Jekyll and Mr. Hyde

The Swiss Family Robinson

The Three Musketeers

The Time Machine

Treasure Island

The Voyages of Doctor Dolittle

The War of the Worlds

White Fang

The Wind in the Willows